NYA'S LONG WALK

A STEP AT A TIME

By
LINDA SUE PARK
NEWBERY MEDALIST

Illustrated by
BRIAN PINKNEY
CORETTA SCOTT KING AWARD WINNER

Clarion Books || Houghton Mifflin Harcourt || Boston New York

Note: Nya's name is pronounced as one syllable: *nyah*.

CLARION BOOKS

3 Park Avenue, New York, New York 10016

Text copyright © 2019 by Linda Sue Park

Illustrations copyright © 2019 by Brian Pinkney

Clarion Books is an imprint of
Houghton Mifflin Harcourt Publishing Company.

HMHBOOKS.COM

The text was set in Grit Primer.

Library of Congress Cataloging-in-Publication Data is available.
ISBN 978-1-328-78133-8

Manufactured in Malaysia
TWP 10 9 8 7 6 5 4 3 2 1
4500761117

To Lynn Malooly,
and to the thousands of students and teachers all over the world who have
donated their time, money, and effort to Water for South Sudan
—L.S.P.

To all the girls of South Sudan who have to walk for water
—B.P.

"Come on," Nya said. "Why are you slow today?"

"I'm tired," Akeer said.

Nya sighed. It was a long way to the water hole. "I'll tell Mama that you were trouble," she said.

"Don't," Akeer begged. "I'll be good." She started walking a little faster.

"Akeer, look!" Nya pointed to the horizon, where she could see a cloud of dust.

"What is it? I can't see," Akeer whined.

Antelope? Or a truck? Too far away to tell. Probably antelope. Trucks were a rare sight in their village.

Akeer was slowing down again. Nya said, "You know the clapping game? Let's sing the song."

"And do the clapping too?"

"Not while we walk. But later, okay?"

At the water hole, they took long drinks. Nya filled the
jerry can. Then they played the clapping game, twice.
"Time to go," Nya said.

Akeer dragged her feet. She walked more and more slowly.
Soon she began to cry, and sat down on the ground.

"I can't walk anymore," she said. "It's too far, and I'm too tired."

"Don't be silly," Nya snapped. "You've walked this before, lots of times."

Akeer cried and snuffled and hiccupped. She looked up at Nya, her eyes very big.

Nya frowned. Akeer was not a crybaby. Usually she skipped along, chattering like a starling.

Nya knelt in front of Akeer and felt her face. Akeer's forehead and cheeks were burning hot. She had stopped crying, and was quiet and still.

Akeer was sick.

Maybe very sick.

Nya felt worry swelling inside her. They were at least half a morning's walk away from home.

I must run and get help, she thought.

She took a few steps, then glanced back at Akeer.

No. She could not leave Akeer alone.

Should they stay and wait for help?

It might be hours before someone came. Akeer would get sicker and sicker.

I will have to carry her. And the water, too.

Her mother would need the water to help make Akeer better.

Nya opened the jerry can and poured out half the water. She picked up the can, hefted its weight, and shook her head.

Still too heavy.

She poured out a little more.

"Akeer?"

Akeer opened her eyes. They were dull and sad.

"I know you don't feel well," Nya said, trying to keep her voice steady, "but you have to climb on my back and hold tight. Can you do that?"

Akeer got on Nya's back. Nya used her headscarf to tie Akeer in place, the way her mother did. Then she picked up the jerry can and began to walk.

Akeer was heavy.

The water was heavy.

Nya could take only a few steps before she had to rest.

Home was so far away! Tears filled Nya's eyes.

I can't do it. It's too far.

Nya saw a tamarind tree up ahead. She swallowed and
blinked away her tears.

I'll go to the tree. I'll put Akeer down there.

When she got to the tree, she thought she might
be able to walk a little more.

Those thorn bushes. I'll rest there.

At the bushes she rested for a moment. Akeer had fallen asleep.

Farther on, Nya saw an old stump.

I can make it to that stump, I know I can.

Step by step, a bit at a time, Nya kept walking.

Outside the village, people came running.

Mama took Akeer. Someone else took the water. Everyone rushed away.

Nya sat down on the ground. She slumped for a long time with her head in her hands, until she heard footsteps coming toward her.

It was Mama.

"We think Akeer has the sickness that comes from drinking dirty water," she said. "She needs to go to the clinic."

It would take Mama two or three days to walk to the clinic. She would have to carry Akeer, as well as food and water for the trip.

"I'll need your help," Mama said.

Nya didn't answer. *I'm so tired. I can't walk anymore today.*

"I know you're tired," Mama said, "but we have to go now."

Nya saw Mama's face, full of worry. She remembered how Akeer had looked, so sad and afraid.

Maybe I can walk a little more. As long as I go a step at a time.

She got to her feet. "When we're at the clinic, I can sing to Akeer," she said, "and play the clapping game with her. She likes that."

Mama nodded and held out her hand. "She is lucky to have you as a sister," she said.

Nya took Mama's hand. Together they went to help Akeer.

AND THEN WHAT HAPPENED?

Akeer got better after a stay in the clinic. She was fortunate: Waterborne diseases are the leading cause of death worldwide for children under the age of five.

The dust cloud Nya saw was indeed a truck. It was being driven by a man named Salva Dut, a former refugee and head of an organization called Water for South Sudan (www.waterforsouthsudan.org).

Eventually, Salva and his crew would install a clean-water well in Nya's village.

The village now has far fewer cases of waterborne illness. And because Nya and the other village girls no longer have to walk hours every day to fetch water, they have time to go to school.

As of 2019, Salva's organization has drilled more than 340 wells serving at least 250,000 people. Students from schools in the US and many other countries have participated in fundraising activities and sponsored 139 of those wells, as well as donating money for a new drilling rig.

Nya and her family are fictional characters, but their story is typical of villagers all over South Sudan.